Blue In Grey

Sylvia Parrow

REDMOND HOUSE

Redmond House

Acknowledgements

Heartfelt thanks to the photographer ISABELLE PERREAU for the cover photos of Paris.

The title is inspired from "Blue in Green" in Miles Davis's magnificent album *Kind of Blue.*

This is a work of fiction. Similarities to real to real people, places, or events are entirely coincidental.

BLUE IN GREY

First Edition. January 14, 2024.

Written by Sylvia Parrow.

ONE

"**WHAT DO YOU MEAN**, deleted?"

"Well, you can't see it there on the screen, can you? So, it means it's probably gone."

"Gone?"

"Maybe something went wrong when you had that extra memory installed, like you said."

All lost!

"Don't tell me you hadn't saved it on a flash drive or something!"

"Never occurred to me."

"Didn't you print out any of it, at least?"

She stares at him blankly. (What's the point, really, of telling her now what she should have done.)

"So what can I do now?" she asks.

"I don't know, Anne," he sighs. "I'm no expert, you know. Are you sure you don't have any of it stored somewhere you've forgotten about?"

She shrugs, still staring at him with the same blank expression.

"I really don't know what else to tell you other than that I'm really sorry."

Anne manages a dry little smile as she opens the door. "Well, thanks anyway. It was very nice of you to stop by."

He hugs her tightly before leaving. "I wish I could have been of more help."

"I know." All of a sudden she can feel the strain of the last seven months embedded in her lower back. But she is still blocking it out of her mind.

Outside, a merciful breeze is slowly diluting the heat. She rushes along the busy avenue and turns into the side street leading to a public garden where she often comes in the evening, for an hour or so right before closing time, to cool from the day's writing in her tiny sweaty *chambre de bonne* under the zinc-sheeted roof.

A few toddlers are still playing in the sandbox, way past their bedtime for sure, but who could blame their mothers—these four women nearby, chatting away in their fluid combination of French and Arabic—for choosing to linger a little longer under the rustling foliage rather than hurry the little ones back to small stuffy apartments. In fact, the park is humming with plenty of blissful lingering tonight, clusters of people on most of the benches all along the slowly darkening alleys, teenagers in twos and threes scattered all over the lawns, and in the central arena a bunch of little kids on small bikes and trikes are revolving around the *kiosque à musique*—one of the quaint fixtures of the garden which, along with the old two-seater gondola swings and the bronze statues of 19th century philanthropists, as well as the tall leafy chestnut trees lining the alleys, gives her favorite *square* its aura of timeless serenity. Two of the young children get off their tiny bicycles and run up the few steps to the bandstand, daring the others to join them in the eerie shadows under the dark roof, and soon they're all running excitedly around the octagonal concrete stage, where tomorrow night local amateur musicians will gather to fête the summer solstice. And every street corner in the city will be jamming too, all night, or at least until the last métros.

And then she'll wait impatiently for the first wave of the ritual summer exodus, when Parisians desert their homes for a whole month sometimes, exercising their French right to long fully-paid vacations.

Then Paris is truly magic.

Tourists still swarm around the city of course, but the pace slackens. All of a sudden there aren't so many people standing in line at the post office or at checkouts, and you gladly find a bit of time on your hands to chat a while with the cashier in the empty grocery store. It is summer and everything slows down, so you might as well slow down too, and you find yourself smiling at everybody—living is so much easier without all those grouchy Parisians.

Except, wasn't it you bickering only last month with that very same friendly cashier because she had overcharged you for a carton of cherry tomatoes that were supposed to be on *offre spéciale* and she lazily pretended not to understand what you were complaining about? And then you snapped at the woman waiting behind you, who was getting impatient as she had to go pick up her children from school, like it was any of your responsibility if the lady couldn't time her daily chores better—well well, haven't you become so Parisian yourself, in spite of your still perceptible foreign accent?

She is smiling at herself now. Yes, Paris without so many people is magic indeed, quicksilver magic, and she will try to make the most of it before the grey clouds of the rainy fall settle over the city again, already missing those long warm summer nights just as they start receding.

Bitter tears suddenly burn her eyes, the first sting of rage. Rage at herself for being so careless again. Outrage at the pathetic joke she keeps turning her life into. But she won't indulge in self-pity, will she? And so she desperately tries to focus her attention on the myriad little scenes that are being played around her—the children in the sandbox, their mothers' lively chat, sparrows hopping chirpily at her feet; dry faded petals whirling down from the thick foliage overhead, riding on a breath of wind for a second of two. Eavesdropping on the genteel conversation from the bench opposite, two old ladies' easy-flowing chitchat about the current heat wave and the soothing coolness of the breeze tonight, and the beautiful flower beds that are so well tended, aren't they; and by the way, have you met the new gentleman garden keeper, isn't he so very nice, and he is from Martinique too, just like his shy stand-offish colleague; oh but he's not so shy, just not the chatty type, you see.

And now forcing her mind to go over all the gems she has been collecting over the months, her memories scattered in every neighborhood throughout the city, like soft deposits of time dust her feet stir up again and again on her long walks around her favorite *quartiers*—starting right here, and with the market street nearby, its daytime bustle of vivid colors and scents, all varieties of spices and herbs, ripe exotic fruit among the seasonal melons and peaches, the briny smell of fresh seafood, and then further down the mouth-watering gusts from the open front of a baker's shop; and the way the street finally bends at a sharp angle to open onto a small secluded *place* nestled against the side of a church in the shade of four plane trees. And of course all the beautiful famous sights of the *ville lumière*, the *quais* along the Seine, the long magnificent perspectives, well of course all the obvious that keeps Paris packed with tourists all year round.

But more than that, yes. Because of the cathedral rising like some protective mother goddess at the core on the small Ile de la Cité. Because from this heart radiates a truly mythic topography: all these streets with their intersections knotting them tightly together, like a maze on an inner map she has been slowly unraveling and deciphering all the time she has spent here, walking half-dreamily, half-searchingly around this city, away from her hometown on some inner quest.

And it suddenly dawns on her, how her long idle walks seem to have been fueling her clumsy plodding through all the chapters of trials and defeats reported page after bitter page, relentlessly, to accumulate all that made-up space of piled-up words between her and all she had meant to get away from. The novel to make articulate sense, somehow, of all that wasted time, all those years of failure and frustration, and plain dumb boredom.

Only to come to this: waste, staring her in the face, once again, sneering at her like an unshakable curse. Precisely when she thought she had made it, she was almost finished with her work, she had come through at last, hadn't she? But right then it had to happen. And how could she have been so careless, so incredibly stupid, once again?

The sandbox is now empty, the old ladies have left too, but the park is still vibrant with gangs of boisterous kids teasing and chasing each other in the benignant dusk. The *gardiens'* whistles will blow any time now and she dreads going back home to her attic room, for what will no doubt be a long sleepless night.

Except that when she does get back home, retracing her steps to the busy avenue, stopping by the Tunisian grocer's store on the corner for something to nibble at in lieu of a late dinner, then climbing wearily up the six flights of stairs, she collapses on the bed and falls asleep right away.

· · · ● ·● · ● ● · ● ·

She wakes up with a start in the middle of the night, her heart racing, trying to retrieve the images that have shaken her in her dream, the one terrible scene that has left a vivid imprint on her consciousness: Notre Dame Cathedral had fallen to pieces in some mysterious cataclysm, its stones, broken sculptures and gargoyles all scattered on the large rectangle of the *parvis*. She was running around like a lunatic, begging the scavengers to leave the holy stones alone so the church could eventually be put together again, but those idiotic thieves wouldn't listen to her, and there were so many of them stealing the precious pieces of Notre Dame. She was frantic with despair but they didn't even seem to care that the cathedral would never be made whole again. Why couldn't they feel her loss?

And now she can't stop sobbing in her bed although she is fully awake. Her head is throbbing mad with a flurry of emotions too slippery for her thoughts to grasp.

Next time she decides to go down for a walk in the 4th or 5th arrondissements (maybe as early as tomorrow as she won't have much of anything else to do, will she?) what magnet will pull her through the intimate entanglement of streets? And if then she strolls on to the Ile de la Cité, if she enters the cathedral as she often would when working out her *redemption*, won't it, like an empty shell, echo nothing but her own dumb emptiness? Since after all she is not Catholic, she doesn't even have any faith to speak of.

And how will she spend the long summer before deciding if it is finally time to go back to the States? But why go back, and to what? Why couldn't she just continue to enjoy her easy clandestine life in the city, walking and gawking around like any regular aficionado?

She knows she won't find the courage to start all over the work that has consumed so much of her energy in the last seven or eight months. Too much has been lost and she couldn't go through the pain of piecing it all together again. Too much suffering involved, too much humiliation and frustration to dredge up, no thanks. What courage she has left will just have to do to help her deal with the fiasco: no meaning to be found, no order to be constructed out of the emotional chaos, no redeeming conclusion and no wisdom in the end—let the rubbles lie in peace, amen.

And to her eyes Paris will wear a new secular face.

And as she lets herself drift off to sleep, the city begins indeed its smooth metamorphosis, releasing itself from the chrysalis of her ersonal myth.

She is now wandering the streets and keeps getting lost, although she's not sure where she's going anyway and it doesn't really feel she is losing her way.

She keeps walking aimlessly in the dark until the first glimmer of dawn peeping in through the skylight shows her a trap door to a darker place underground, where she can now rest at last.

· · · ● · ● ● · · ·

Daylight is flooding in through the open skylight, along with the discordant blare of an electric guitar. Ah yes, she recalls on opening her eyes, *la fête de la musique.* Probably the *concierge*'s teenage son tuning up his instrument in the courtyard below as the big party is slowly getting under way. If he's up, it must be pretty late!

A quick glance at the clock on her bedside table tells her it is in fact past 10. How could she have overslept? On an empty stomach too—as she remembers skipping dinner the night before.

And then remembers, as among the hunger pangs she feels another, duller pain tightening her abdomen, why she didn't bother to set the alarm before going to bed.

She moves a tentative foot into the hot shaft of sunlight under the small blue rectangle cut out of the roof. So hot already. Extricating herself from the low alcove where her bed lies tucked in under the sloping roof, she switches on her trusty old fan.

As the blades start purring softly, churning the stagnant air, all the details of the previous day's shock start trickling back into her consciousness. She isn't blocking anything out anymore, letting the whole thing flood her mind. Only wondering why she can't feel her pulse quicken in the full recollection. But no, she just sits there in the droning stillness that manages to keep at bay the electric screeches downstairs; somehow drained of her rage. Maybe still too drowsy to feel any rage or pain? Numbed, in any case. Watching like in a trance the motes of dust stir and glitter in the blinding light under the skylight. Just wondering where all the rage and despair might have gone.

Until the metallic singsong of her cellphone jolts her out of her numbness.

"Allooo? Anne? I wake you up? Nooo?" Her boss-cum-landlady's seductive lilt.

"Hello Laure. Of course you're not waking me up. How are you?"

"Sorry, I know you're very busy with your writing, but I have a big, big problem. You know the girls eat lunch at school, yes? But today the women who serve the food, they are—how do you say it in English already? *en grève?*"

"You mean the cafeteria staff's on strike."

"Exactly. Can you believe it?"

(Jesus, lady, how could I *not* believe it? What could be more French than striking, besides *baguette* and *croissants*?)

"Would you like me to have lunch with them?"

"Could you do that? Oh Anne, that would be so, sooo nice of you! Could you fetch them at school first?"

"Sure, what time?"

"You must be there at 11:30, is it okay?"

"I'll be there."

"And you can bring them back to school after? Yes? At 13:30?"

"Of course, I'll take good care of them, don't worry."

(What are undeclared tenants/employees for, if not for being utterly dependable whatever the circumstances?)

"Okay, so don't forget, 11:30. Thank you so, very, very, much. You are doing me a big, big service. You see, I can't just leave my job like that today."

Unlike poor jobless me, who don't even have any real work to keep me busy at this point, Anne winces. In fact, this strike is almost like a godsend.

· · · ● · ● · ● · ·

Pauline is already out when Anne reaches the school gate, chatting among a gaggle of chirpy little girls. Her younger sister is just coming down the steps with her own bubbly batch of kids. Anne waves and calls out to them to grab their attention out of the cheerful chaos where several other grown-ups are also rounding up their own charges.

"*Hé Anne, c'est toi qui t'occupes de nous aujourd'hui? Cool!*"

"Yep, it's party time girls. And I'll take you to the *Macdo* if you promise to keep it a secret."

They grin at her joke, relishing the pretend conspiracy. There's a strict ban on fast food in Laure's health-conscious and ecologically-correct household, but this is no day for culinary niceties.

"You'll also have to promise to speak only English during the whole meal."

"No problemo!" Pauline promises.

And why should there be any? These kids have been raised mostly by English-speaking au pairs since they were babies. Now, as times are fast a-changing, they also have a Chinese babysitter who can teach them some Mandarin—besides the American private tutor who can occasionally double up as an extra nanny at extra short notice and no extra cost.

"No problemo!" echoes Jeanne. And this feisty first-grader proceeds to tell Anne all about her eventful morning in perfectly fluent English. First, her (SO strict and mean!) teacher decided to move her to a different seat because she was supposedly getting too chummy with her neighbor as she let him cheat off her during the dictation (BIG deal!). So now she has to sit up front next to a dull goofy girl (whose name she can't be bothered to memorize), and is forbidden to turn around (EVER!) and take even a little peep at what is going on with the rest of the class, so she is bound to be missing out on a lot of fun stuff. Then her best buddy Louise was not allowed (AGAIN!) to go out and play during recess. And to top it all, Mehdi, one of the most fun members of her posse, announced he was moving away soon to somewhere in the suburbs.

"That was a pretty tough morning all right," Anne nods.

"But you know, Jeanne," Pauline lectures big-sisterly, "Madame Martin is only trying to help you concentrate better on your work, so you can really apply yourself."

Jeanne shrugs. "Mom and Dad say they're not worried about my grades."

"Do you really think they mean it?"

They have naturally reverted to French when addressing each other and Anne is about to remind them of their promise, but they are now standing in line to order their happy meals and the restaurant is buzzing with overexcited children from the same school who just can't believe their luck: it seems like every parent or babysitter here has chosen to make a special occasion of the strike. So Anne lets the girls chat with their friends for a while before leading them to a somewhat isolated table upstairs where they can resume their English-only conversation in peace. That's how conscientious she is as a tutor.

"Why can't we eat with Juliette and Luna?" Pauline complains.

"Because I want you guys to talk to me, not to your schoolmates. Don't you have anything new to tell me?"

"You have to come and see the kittens again before we give them away," Jeanne volunteers.

"Mom says we can keep one, though," Pauline adds. "I'd like to keep the little black one, she's the cutest."

"Okay, but I get to choose her name," the little sister replies. Which she chooses in a split second: "We'll call her Mehdi."

"You know Mom doesn't like us calling pets after human people."

"Mom doesn't have to know about it, except if somebody tells her!" (looking sideways at her big sister). "We'll give her another name for when Mom's around, that's all. You get to choose it if you want."

Jeanne is actually pretty good at this little game. She once christened a hamster Bernard after the grandfather who had given it to her for her birthday. When Laure objected, the little girl pretended to comply with her mother's diktat by renaming the furry little creature Fifi or some other more appropriately goofy name. But he was still Bernard behind closed doors, his underground identity as it were, in loyal homage to the beloved grandpa.

"Anyway, Mehdi's a name for a boy, not for a girl", Pauline says.

He little sister rolls her eyes in her distinctive droll fashion. "She's a cat, what does she care? Nobody will make fun of her, I don't think!"

They have reverted back to French again.

"Don't you think having two names might confuse your kitten?" the conscientious tutor cuts in to steer them back to English.

"Duh!" (another theatrical rolling of the eyes). "My father calls me *Moustique* sometimes, I'm not confused, am I?"

"Good point, but you're a smart little girl."

"So? Cats are pretty smart too!"

The older sister shakes her head in disbelief. "You sure are a weirdo!"

"*You*'re the fruitcake," comes the retort, in English still. "You're *fruitcakier* than anybody else I know!"

And the girls now launch into a jubilant joust of imaginative insults in both languages while nibbling away at their french fries.

• • • ● • ● • • •

She's got to be the *humptiest dumptiest* of them all and somehow it doesn't affect her all that much. It is at least eight and since she took the girls back to school, she has been doing nothing but lie on her bed, looking at the blue rectangle in the roof and the light beams shifting stealthily across the floor. Thinking, dozing off, even dreaming maybe.

She thought at first she just needed a digestive nap. She hardly ever eats meat, let alone a burger with fries! But she ended up letting the whole afternoon slip by. Sounds come up to her through the open skylight. A faraway jazzy tune from the avenue, and much closer, the merry racket of a get-together in the courtyard below, laughter and clattering dishes floating up to her. Firecrackers, horns blowing in the thickening traffic. Sudden shouts from a nearby window, some anger lashing out. And again bursts of laughter from the courtyard. The usual mess of life.

She is listening, her ears and nostrils taking in what her eyes can't see. Feeling like she's been touched by something like—what, peace? "Grace, even"? Some small quicksilver measure of it, at least.

And suddenly all she can make out of the deepening blue in the skylight is the violet shade of Jeanne's eyes, this lily of a little girl as she turned up her face to say good bye, blinking in the bright sunshine, "thank you for the happy meal, it was SO cool! The lightness in her small pale face, at once so delicate and bold.

A faint knock on the door. She doesn't budge, half asleep. Then comes another one, a harder clearer rap this time.

"Anne, it's me, Matt. Are you there?"

She unbolts the door. "Sorry Matt, I wasn't expecting you. You know the lowlife crowd around here." Squatters mostly, harmless young drifters, but they can be real leeches sometimes and she's tired of playing friendly neighbor.

"You can never be too careful with these potheads, that's for sure," Matt agrees, stepping in. And he should know. He used to rent one of those dozen tiny *chambres de bonnes* all clustered together at the topmost floor, right under the zinc roof of this typical Hausmannian building. But then he moved out two months ago to settle down with his French girlfriend in a more suitable two-room apartment, a few blocks further down the avenue.

"Should've phoned before coming up, I know. Just wanted to check in on you."

"I'm fine, thanks. And it's always great to see you!"

"Did you manage to retrieve your writing?"

"Nope. As you said, it was probably deleted accidentally at the computer place."

"I'm really sorry to hear that. But listen, it can't just have completely vanished like that. Go back to the computer place so they can help you retrieve it."

"Don't worry. I've decided to just let it go."

"What do you mean? After all the work you've put into this! Come on Anne, I'm sure you can remember most of it, at least."

"Well, might as well forget all about it. I'm through with it."

He looks at her with a frown of concern, unsure how to react--very sweet.

"Look, I'm fine, really. I feel so much lighter, actually. The truth is, it might very well turn out to be a blessing in disguise."

"If you say so," he shrugs. Then draws her closer for a big bear hug.

"Why don't we go for a walk around the neighborhood, hear a bit of music, you know? Maybe have a glass in our old café, for old times' sake. What do you say?" He's not so much offering as begging.

"What is Bérengère doing tonight?" Anne asks as casually as possible as they start walking down the corridor towards the stairs.

"Her mother's in town. They went out to a restaurant. They have some catching up to do, so I figured, better get out of their hair.

Then, as they start climbing down the narrow staircase, he suddenly grabs her arm.

"You know, Bérengère and I are planning to get married soon."

"Congratulations!" she cheers, but a sharp squeeze on her forearm puts a quick stop to her perfunctory show of excitement.

"Of course, I have to prove to her folks I can be a dependable breadwinner. Her father is a doctor, you know." Frowning to convey the sense of pressure his in-laws-to-be have already managed to put on him so he won't disgrace the family. "Fortunately, I've just been asked to teach more English classes at the Institute , so—"

"I'm sure it will be easier to get a better job once you've married Bérengère and are eligible for citizenship."

"Right. Of course. I don't mind teaching anyway. Only it's so time-consuming once you start worrying about making real bucks. And of course I want to keep some free time for my photography, you know. But believe me, that free time is dwindling away fast. Not to mention the space. Now that I am sharing an apartment with Bérengère, I can't be too messy. Of course we're both making tremendous efforts, until we can afford to move into a bigger place."

Of course, of course... But Anne knows better than to open her big jaded mouth. So she nods instead, probably a little too vigorously. The smell of serious trouble brewing is unmistakable. Here is a young foolish guy (six years her junior) who for some reason thinks he's found the right girl. Well, let him be. Who knows, it might work out fine after all. Who is she to tell? He keeps silent too as they come down the few remaining steps.

Once in the lobby, Matt can't refrain from peeping into the courtyard where the party is still going strong. "Let me say a quick hello to Madame Pereira Gonçalves before we get out."

And watching him chat and joke with the matronly Portuguese *concierge* who greets him with cheers of joyful surprise, Anne realizes how much he probably misses his old life already. Isn't this all going too fast for him, this settling down to order and stability, all this planning for marriagedom? Come on, how exciting can the prospects be? What's wrong with the guy anyway, it doesn't take

ESP to figure out what's awaiting him behind the hairpin bend! A U-turn back to suburban America, except for the French décor, that's what he's headed for.

The sad thing is, she doesn't recall Matt ever feeling lonely when he lived all by himself in his tiny messy room, sometimes without coming out of it for several days in a row. Garrulous, sociable most of the time, mercurial really. Working hard on his photography when it suited him, taking his time. His own man. Why did he have to fall head over heels for that particular girl? She's sweet, sure, but what can she really understand about Matt?

Well of course, Anne knows she might be misjudging Bérengère. But she seems so young, so spoiled and immature. How could she even start to understand what it took for a guy like Matt to leave everything behind him in the States—career, comfort, close relations and all, ad-libbing his own expat lifestyle here, some cross between Thoreau and Hemingway: *I went to Paris, France because I wished to live deliberately. Paris indeed was always worth it and you received return for whatever you brought to it. Simplify, simplify, and suck out all the marrow of life.* No status, no social security number, no lofty ambition, nothing to distract you from the simple essential necessities of food and shelter, and then all the time that's left unfrittered.

But wait, who says that's really Matt in the end? Her idealistic rendition of him, rather. Her own faltering aspirations projected onto him, poor soul, who might just be really ready to settle down and turn fully legal here.

They wander aimlessly down the avenue, venturing into some side streets where youthful rock groups have taken over the sidewalks; meandering toward their old favorite café where they finally end up stopping for drinks. The mood here is R&B, more to their liking. Matt gets into the swing of the party, beating out the rhythm with his hands and feet and his whole swaying body. Anne's obvious lack of perkiness annoys him, though. He pulls her out of her chair to get her to dance with him. Waltzing her across the small dance floor still when the music has gotten more sedate, he announces, point-blank: "By the way, I want you to be my best man at the wedding."

"Cute!"

"I mean it. You're my only real friend here, you know."

"I'll be honored."

And she truly is. And she inwardly gives him her blessings after all.

The R&B band steps down the makeshift stage, replaced by a decent enough amateur jazz quartet that barely manage to cram themselves and their instruments into the tiny space. Luckily, many people have left already because tomorrow is a regular working day. The few remaining patrons huddle around the musicians, all swathed together in a thick blanket of cigarette smoke, lulled by the blue drift of an elegiac sax impro. The trumpet picks up the theme, expands on it to give it more body, lets it flesh out and spread into a prismatic burst of lyrical effusion, and soar, and thin out finally to its reedy paroxysm, die out in midair, unresolved; wisps of smoke curling up iridescent in the afterglow.

Eager applause breaking up the collective trance.

Then the tempo speeds up. At first she tries hard to keep up with it, it goes so fast, faster and faster, and she's trying to catch on to the bass, with the simple basic tune flitting wildly about the beat, variations reeling at the edge of the melody, leaping off the track and across the gaps they tear into the melodic line, looping back into it light and nimble, and she finally manages to, she jumps into the rhythm, yes, ecstatic, she made it, she got it, she is weightless, blowing with the horns, drums crashing and rolling the beat, bass keeping it up, Matt rocking in it too, blown away, weightless.

• • • • ● • ● • • • •

Again she's been walking all night through her dreams. Only this time, smart girl, she wasn't going to lose her way as she thought of dropping a pebble after each and every step she took. But when suddenly she found herself at the top of a hill, looking down, the pebbles had become tiny grains of sand strewn all around, shimmering in the technicolor sunlight. Rippling away in bright convolutions all around her feet and as far as her eyes could see.

Then a sudden gust of wind swept across the sands, scattering them all to the four corners.

The blank sheets of paper that had been lying around on her desk fluttered madly about for a few seconds. Lightning flashed concomitantly with a crash of thunder. She managed to close the skylight right before the rain started pelting the pane.

A violent storm threshing the roof and she in the eye of it, wide awake and fiercely determined. No more lying, drifting, shirking. No more.

• • • • ● • ● • • • •

When a few days later, as she is about to type a letter, she opens an icon on the desktop and finds hiding inside her correspondence file another misplaced icon, it truly feels like a ghost has introduced itself into her computer.

For a few seconds she looks in shock at this apparition: the novel that she thought had been lost accidentally.

Then she drags it to the basket icon at the bottom of the screen and hastens to empty the trash.

A few clicks, that's all it took. Just a few clicks of the mouse to get rid of excess emotional baggage, which, let's face it, could never have added up to any redemptive "mandala" or whatever she had meant it to be.

Give it up, already. And get a life, at last.

And the taste of freedom, tangy like a sour apple.

TWO

"SO WHAT DO YOU think, when should I start addressing either of them as *tu*? They're much older, I don't want to be disrespectful. But then they're not strangers anymore, so-"

"Gee Matt, how am I supposed to know that?"

"Well, you've been around here longer than I have, haven't you?"

"So what?" Anne shrugs. "How does that make me an expert in French arcane etiquette?" Then patting his hand with mock-empathy. "I say, just refrain from addressing them altogether."

Which is funny, come to think of it, since that's exactly what he's been doing. "But I can't keep doing this forever, can I? I'm marrying their daughter, for crying out loud. Sooner or later I'm gonna have to find a way of acknowledging their presence!"

"Well, that's a toughie," she nods, looking around to try and catch the waiter's attention. And then again the dismissive shrug: "Why don't you just call it off?"

"What, the wedding, you mean?"

"Why do you guys have to get married all of a sudden anyway?"

End of story as far as she is concerned. But how could he blame her? Why should she even care to understand the mess he's gotten himself into? When his own mind is sure giving him no clear hint on how to negotiate the situation.

It all just happened so fast. Six months ago, Bérengère was just another cool classy girl hanging around their favorite café. Or rather, to be precise, one in a trio of sexy actresses rehearsing at the time, in the small cozy theatre of the nearby *centre culturel*, a witty little comedy by a young aspiring playwright/director, who was also playing off-stage his own version of Pygmalion with two of his Thespian *protégées*. The third girl, Bérengère, clearly the most independent of the three, Matt had decided to try his luck with. He managed, easily enough, to get her to date him—what with his easy-go-funky attitude and exotic Yankee twang. And they hit it off right away; were having a fine easy dandy time of it actually, when for some obscure reason, after only a few weeks, they had to get all serious about it. Which, to be quite honest, was mostly his own doing, as all of a sudden, out of nowhere, he found himself blurting out a proposal to her.

Well, sort of.

It all flared up on a crisp Sunday morning in early March—forever stamped in his memory, to be sure: Bérengère wrapped in his old bathrobe, sitting on the edge of his futon and bending over a newspaper spread out on the floor under the skylight; her long chestnut hair flowing loose down her left cheek, one single lock curling on her neck—so graceful and delicate she moved him and turned him on all at once. He crawled up to her from the other side of the bed where he had been reclining in a blissful half-drowsy state, and toppled her backwards, but instead of fighting him off in a playful struggle as he had half-expected—she could be such a fun rough player for all her classy sophistication—she let him move over her pliant flesh, without even protesting that he was not wearing a condom; urging him on as he was making love to her with an eagerness he couldn't remember ever hearing before. Then as her body lay soft and sweaty against his, the faintest whisper in his right ear: "What if I fall pregnant?"—she said *fall* because that's the literal translation of the verb they use in French, *tomber enceinte*, but it sounded so quaint and erotic in her cute little accent, he could only beam an ecstatic smile in her flushed face: "It's all right, I'll marry you." MARRY! And there he was with the big goofy smile plastered across his face, vaguely aware of the panic failing to kick up a racket inside his numb skull.

Well, she didn't *fall* pregnant after all. And boy was he meticulous about his prophylactic routine after that! But somehow, the deal was clinched. And the truth is, to his own amazement, he found himself playing along with it: the being-a-couple, holding hands and interlocking fingers, the smooching nonstop, gooey smiles and tittering under the envious stares of her girlfriends; not to mention the distinctive glint of irony in his own buddies' eyes—especially Anne's here. He endured it all with good humor and snuggled into this all-new feel-good intimacy.

Until he met her parents. A bitch of a wake-up call that was, the right fix to jolt him clear out of snug blissyland. Not that he shouldn't have anticipated the shock—Bérengère's classy distinction had to originate somewhere, obviously.

So here was doting Papa, *le docteur Beaufort*, who turned out to be a nice enough fellow, actually (*"Mais appelez-moi donc Jacques, voyons!"*). Eyeing *notre jeune ami américain* a little suspiciously though, or maybe just skeptically; wondering no doubt how long this new crush of his daughter's would last. And of course here

was also gorgeous, definitely high-strung Maman (who, inciden-
tally, did not volunteer to be called anything at all). The lady's
smoldering spite didn't take very long to break through her impeccable varnish of Gallic good manners. It didn't help matters
in the least when Bérengère, with her very own offbeat sense of
timing, announced point-blank right in the middle of the Sunday
lunch that she had interrupted her university studies for a while so
she might direct more of her energies to the protracted launching
of her acting career. Out darted to Matt an unmistakable flash of
anger from Maman's delicate-featured scowl. Woah, what was that
all about, the poor wretch could only wonder while choking on
a morsel of *boeuf bourguignon*. Sedate Papa, always the debonair,
calmly suggested to his darling impractical daughter that, *bon*, she
might perhaps consider sticking it out at the Sorbonne, as that was
surely a safer bet on a future career than the acting studio, wasn't it;
and *voyons* anyway, couldn't she just continue to juggle both acts
for a little while longer, *enfin quoi*, let's be sensible here, shall we,
pour l'amour du ciel? Poor Matt wondered if this wasn't his cue to
add in his two cents of wisdom, and detach himself in no uncertain
terms from his sweetheart's impulsive whim; stealing instead an
uneasy glance at Maman, and deciding in a split second on remaining tight-lipped and busily chewing all through the remainder of
the seven-course meal.

Whatever quota of faux pas tolerance he had been granted, he
soon exceeded, that's for sure. All he could try to do then was
fumble his hapless way around his soon-to-be in-laws without
aggravating them any more than was strictly unavoidable. Which
seemed to suit them fine enough. So, so far so good, sort of.

Still, how should he address them?

Anne has finally managed to get the waiter's attention. The glass of icy beer and lemonade *panaché* he sets down in front of her on the small round bistro table soon pacifies her grumpy mood.

"There's always another option for a helpless non-native such as yourself: mess up the conjugations so much they won't be able to figure out in the end if you're saying *tu* or *vous*."

She takes a long anticipated sip and grins broadly at him. At least she managed to get a crack of a smile out of him.

"Believe me, these people aren't the type that will look kindly on a clumsy Yankee fucking up their language."

But he is grinning back, lighting up at the huge cup of vanilla ice cream doused in caramel coulis she has ordered for him as a special cheer-up treat.

"What does Bérengère advise you to do?"

"She just laughs it off. 'Who cares?' she says. 'Just be yourself,' she says."

He snorts, then dips into the mound of cream, scooping out a generous spoonful. Beaming now like a kid on Christmas day.

"I don't think she has a clue, to tell you the truth."

"What you should call her parents, you mean?"

"How I should relate to them at all."

Another luscious scoop vanishes into his mouth; his taste buds register the caramel melting in with the cold vanilla, sliding down his throat.

"In any case, she doesn't seem to think they deserve being humored all that much."

Another scoop, another boost to his frayed morale.

He holds his spoon halfway up for a few seconds and emits a gurgling chuckle.

"To tell you the truth, I don't think the French themselves have much of a clue how they should address each other most of the time."

THREE

O NE HOUR TO KILL before the stupid meeting at seven.

She's been busy cleaning up and sorting things out, dusting, scrubbing, discarding, and she is now sitting, showered and refreshed, in the one armchair right in the middle of the un-cluttered space, letting her skin dry in the long cool drafts blowing in from the open skylight.

She feels quite pleased with herself as she scans the tidy little room once again. Only the bare necessities of modern comfort have been granted her *chambre de bonne* and she intends to keep it that way, spare and clean. Next to the shower tub in a corner, the white porcelain sink and then the kitchen nook with the tiny fridge, the two-burner hot plate and the small cupboard chock-full of mispatched dishes left by former occupants. Then the bed tucked under the sloping roof. Against the other wall slanting up to the door, an old bulky wardrobe, however they managed to haul it up here, and her pinewood shelves, the only item of furniture she purchased herself, now cleared of all the notebooks and papers that had been piling up and gathering dust in the last few months. The small desk stands out under the skylight, next to the comfortable armchair wrapped in a lavender blue quilt, the only touch of softness in the room, and a larger table near the door, with two old wooden chairs and a stool that occasionally serves as a bedside table. Want but little.

But why on earth didn't she decline to meet this guy?

Two big garbage bags are waiting out in the corridor. One bulging with unrecyclable junk she'll dispose of in the regular *poubelle*, the other left open, with all her notes to be tossed into the recycle bin. Better take them down before one of the nosy busy-bodies around here gets the freaky notion of rummaging through her old papers. One last critical look around her little cell before double-locking the door, and off she goes, hurrying along the dark spooky corridor, past the shared squat-down toilet whose door for some obnoxious reason is always gaping unchained, and down the winding stairs, with her two cumbersome bags of waste on her back.

· · · ● · ● · ● · · ·

She is walking briskly down the bustling avenue rank with the exhaust fumes of rush hour traffic, then turns into a long narrow street that shoots diagonally across the neighborhood. Here is the real backbone of this peripheral *quartier* squeezed into a quasi perfect triangle between the *périphérique* beltway and the two main arteries branching off into the northern suburbs. A fast-moving crowd is pushing along the thin strip of the sidewalk, people loaded with grocery bags, children of all colors and shades in tow, steering strollers around the typical dog feces and spouting a staccato string of practical talk into their cell phones.

She just moves along, keeping pace with this anonymous rush hour flow. Well, not all that anonymous maybe, as so many faces she recognizes from seeing them around here countless times. So many faces that recognize her too no doubt, give her some hint of recognition even sometimes, just a flicker of a smile, or so it seems, as she passes by. Even a nod occasionally, like from the Tamil guy standing in the doorway of his small *taxiphone/cybercafé*, which Anne, having no internet connection in her nest, patronizes on a regular basis.

She has reached a special corner and slows down her pace instinctively. Because standing still for half a second in the middle of the side street she's now crossing, she can see, craning its neck in the hazy distance above and between the grey roofs, the tiny Eiffel Tower, inconspicuous if you go by too fast. Here on Bastille Night last year she came across an Asian family who had also thought of coming to this quiet spot away from the big crowds on the Champ de Mars or the Butte Montmartre to catch something of the fireworks, the three shy children huddled together, whispering their ooohs and aaahhs in unison. She remembers wondering where exactly they could have come from, if they were *clandestins* too—of course no dilettantes like herself. It certainly felt so as she stood there with them for a few minutes in the quiet street, grasping on the sly their tiny intimate portion of the *fête nationale*.

Through the window of the pharmacy at the angle her eyes meet those of a little girl that she actually seems to know—yes, she remembers her, who waves at her now, a kid she's been asked a few times to babysit along with Pauline and Jeanne—what's her name though? Anne waves back and the girl turns away. A mere

two-second gaze of acknowledgement that gave her an ounce more
substance.

She needs to collect her thoughts and figure out what she can
tell this guy she's supposed to meet in about twenty minutes. Here
she is already standing in front of the café, but she decides against
sitting down on the crowded terrace on the sidewalk. She slows
down her pace, hesitates in front of the gate into a long narrow
square. Just tell him the simple honest truth. Sure, I thought I was
writing something, but the whole thing turned out to be a joke.
It's quite embarrassing, but what else is there to say? When Matt
told you about me I guess I was still one of those expat artists or
wannabes you probably write about in your column, or whatever
it is you want to interview me for. But this is all over now.

Absent-mindedly she's retraced her steps back to the café and
spots a free table on the edge of the terrace. Settles down, shifting
on the chair to dodge the cigarette smoke from the next table.

This was all so ridiculous anyway, this expat writer business of
mine. So phony in the end. Like, seriously, can you imagine me
sitting at, say, this here tiny round metal table on this cramped
semblance of a terrace, and actually getting inspiration from, like,
the ebb and flow of this passing crowd? Trying to get hold of
my very own genuine Paris experience? Although actually that
was definitely not what I was after. Paris in my case just became
the blurry setting to an illusory quest for light, or redemption, or
whatever it was I imagined it to be, that took me nowhere but
around and back through the same old obsessions. Well, I ain't no
writer after all, and that's that. And I have no idea what I'm doing
here in the end. Except, I shouldn't even be here in the first place,
but oddly enough, it somehow helps me feel more alive and free

to live among all this contingency. What decadent self-indulgence, wouldn't you say?

A woman has come up to her, looks intently into her eyes. "Anne?"

"Yes?"

She grabs a chair from a nearby table and sits down. The terrace feels even more cramped. What the hell does she think…?

"I'm Frankie," she explains.

For some reason, Anne had expected Frankie to be a man, a young guy like Matt probably. But here is a woman, about her age too. And she keeps staring at Anne with her strange inquisitive squint and lopsided smile.

"You don't recognize me, do you?"

What? Anne really looks at the woman now, searchingly. She can vaguely feel she should make something out of these features, as she's definitely seen this face somewhere.

"You know, I asked Matt not to tell you my full name so it would be a surprise! But here we are and you don't have a clue who I am!" she quips with a mock frown.

"I know I definitely know you from somewhere…"

"Frankie! Frances McDowell! Doesn't it ring a bell?"

A surge of long-buried memories suddenly flood back.

"Frankie! Wow!"

The shock is so sharp she's almost speechless, reeling with disbelief. How small can the world get on you?

"Matt keeps telling me about this great friend of his, this American writer, a Bryn Mawrter too, I kinda intuited who he was talking about before he even told me your name, for some uncanny reason.

Obviously, you made more of an impression on me than I did on you back then!"

The ironic grin is familiar all right. It almost feels like Frankie's jumped right out of the twilight zone. That's how much Anne realizes she's insulated herself, she's so totally blocked out that era of her past in particular. And she still can't figure out anything intelligent or nice to say.

Frankie bursts out laughing. "Well, *I* at least am delighted to see you again!"

And she does seem so. A powerful surge of long-forgotten emotions now bring her into sharp focus: Frankie, the French major in the gang Anne hung out with in her senior year, all these smart cocksure girls (young *women,* sorry!) who had such grand plans for their glorious future ahead. What reason did she have to block her out of her memory, though? They both lived in the French House, where they could practice their French daily. Anne was just back from her junior year in Paris and Frankie became the gossamer thread to all the freedom and insouciance she had experienced there—here, that is.

And here she is again, after a whole lot of murky waters have flown under the bridges on either side of the Atlantic. She has aged and wised up too, no doubt. Although the spark of gleeful irony hasn't dulled in her bright blue eyes, the crow's feet at their corners only seem to bring it out more brightly. She doesn't look defeated in the least. What can she read out of the lines and shadows under the eyes facing her own?

"It's been such a long time," Anne manages to say at last. "What have you been doing with yourself all these years?"

"Hard to sum up a whole decade!"

"Didn't you go to Penn after we graduated from Bryn Mawr?"

"You do remember me after all!" Frankie beams. "That's right, I did! And I met a cute French student there, ended up getting married, moved here, had two kids. What about yourself? How's your novel coming along? Matt told me you're almost finished with it."

"How come you know Matt?" Anne dodges.

"I'm his boss at the Institute."

"Do you think he can earn a decent salary teaching there on a more regular basis?"

"As long as he puts in the right amount of hours," Frankie shrugs. "He's actually a very good teacher. But tell me about yourself!"

The waiter's interruption is a welcome break to Anne who needs to gather her thoughts.

"So tell me, how's your novel coming along?"

"Well, it's not actually. It's not coming along at all. I had to terminate it."

Anne got her old friend confused all right, so now she can't shirk explaining how she thought she could hide out here to write her redemption—seriously! How she kept herself busy with this long thick patchwork of words and pathos, the longer and thicker the cocoon, the better. Until she finally got to know better.

Frankie is palpably uncomfortable, wondering of course what could have gone so wrong in her old college buddy's life.

"Pretty much everything as soon as I graduated from college, really. Settled in the wrong place to get the wrong job, married the wrong guy, morphed into the wrong person," Anne hears herself confess.

She looks away from Frankie's puzzled frown to the east where a menacing cumulonimbus has gathered over the grey roofs and the Sacré Coeur's chalk-white dome in the distance. Did she remember to close the skylight? The question keeps her distracted for a few seconds while the waiter comes back with their drinks.

Frankie unwraps her sugar cubes and stirs them slowly into her jasmine tea.

"Of course it's not all that bleak, I'm just giving you the gist of it," Anne blunders on, lifting her glass to her lips with as much cool as she can summon up. "Anyway, I guess I can put all this mess behind me now and finally simplify my life for real."

Hard not to smile at how trite she can hear herself sounding. Is that all it comes down to in the end, for God's sake, this premature midlife crisis of hers, just a bunch of sorry clichés?

Frankie smiles back. "Simplify... I remember that came first on your list even back then."

"Ouch," Anne winces in an effort at self-mockery. "Well, I guess I haven't really gotten around to that stage yet, seeing as I've done nothing much so far but complicate my life in a big way. " She can't help laughing a little. "I'm way off course, in fact."

Frankie feels free to smile more broadly now. They are definitely back on more comfortable ground.

"Still, my *chambre de bonne* is pretty spartan, real tiny too, like some little cabin up in the air."

Frankie grabs Anne's hand across the table. "You know, I've really missed you all these years. Why didn't you keep in touch with the gals? We were pretty close," she insists. And she clearly means the two of them in particular. It was indeed an intense friendship basking in the afterglow of Anne's Paris experience. She secretly felt her junior year here had been her own secular version of a vision quest. She was still high on it when back in college she started hanging out with Frankie, who was so bright and brilliant, so outgoing, confident and sunny in a way Anne couldn't hope to be. Maybe by exposing herself to this bright girl's light she wouldn't be tempted to shrink back into her old shell, as she had so often been accused of doing, and betray her vision.

Yet by the end of the first term Frankie' brightness had started to dim somehow. Had turned out to be only superficial shininess, her myriad eccentricities mere ordinary flaws. Anne hated her friend for letting her down like that. Hated herself even more for being so unfair and ridiculous. They remained good enough friends until graduation though.

By the end of the second term, Anne's dream vision had started to pale in the harsh light of reality, as she had had to make no-nonsense plans for a summer job and then the rest of her life. When she graduated she knew for a fact she wouldn't be likely to keep in touch with Frankie, or any girl of the gang for that matter—her happy college days were definitely over.

She desperately wants to shift the attention away from herself, so she starts shooting a volley of questions about Frankie's life—job, kids, husband, house, hobbies, family back home in the States and the whole nine yards, she suddenly wants to know it all, and Frankie readily obliges with all the particulars. Not that Anne is listening all that carefully. But she's watching Frankie intently as she's talking to her, mesmerized by her old friend's effortless assurance, the graceful ease with which she seems to have fit into this life she's telling her all about. She is not envious—no, not in the least, and this is no self-delusion on her part. This is all too alien to her, all this comfortable self-confidence and adequacy. But a strange notion hits her, inarticulate, nonsensical really, yet somehow compelling, that they might just be two sides of the same coin. *"Que tu es lunatique!"* she remembers Frankie jabbing at her once, back then. Which doesn't mean 'crazy' in French, a subtlety Anne failed to grasp at the time. Indeed she would sometimes withdraw away from everybody to hide and sulk in that quiet shell of hers. Moody all right. Then Frankie would look in vain for her own radiance shining off her friend's blander face. For what was Anne to her other than another satellite? But now with her husband and kids and comfortable lifestyle she is in the end what poor Anne can't be, and above all, won't ever have to bother to be, since she is living that out for them both, somehow, and her friend can crouch moodily where *she* won't ever have to bother to go, under the coin, face down.

Woah, the *kir royal* Anne is ingesting on a practically empty stomach must be messing up her mind, Anne realizes. Her emotions too, as her mood suddenly shifts and she finds herself waxing garrulous. She now becomes animated, gesturing wildly, speaking with her hands like a regular extrovert, Mediterranean style. With her right hand rather, the other coyly wrapped around the glass she's still nursing.

When the first rain drops hit the sidewalk, they ran down the block to a seafood restaurant, holding hands and laughing hysterically. They reminisced, gossiped, confided over a platter of fresh oysters and a bottle of Chardonnay. Anne's wine-enhanced ambivalence dissolving in the warm rainy night when they hurried afterwards to the nearest métro station. "Let's promise we'll keep

in touch," Frankie urged, then turned away and vanished down
the stairs to the platform.

• • • • ● • ● • • •

Climbing up the six flights of stairs somewhat clears up Anne's
mind, although she still feels restless and overexcited, unable for
sure to lie down and get to sleep. So she settles down in the armchair under the solid black rectangle of the skylight, which thank
god turned out to be closed after all. Swathing herself in the soft
lavender blue quilt, with a genuine all-American legal pad poised
on her knees, and a pen she plies across the neatly lined expanse of
the yellow paper. Although she can't really write anything.

FOUR

T HERE IS THIS HOMELESS man she sometimes says hello to, and she will occasionally give him the change in her pocket. When he can recognize her, that is—he is often sprawled out on the sidewalk in a semi-comatose state. But once, in the métro, she got to hear his sad story. He came up to her that day to ask for a euro or two. She shook her head but instead of moving on to the next passenger in the thick line waiting along the platform, he kept blinking his one rheumy eye at her, and cursed her for not giving him anything. Instead of ignoring him, she explained that she simply had no change at all to give him at that particular moment. Noticing her accent, he asked her where she was from. The next day he might be unable to recognize her when she crossed his path again, already far too drunk by then, but that morning in the métro his mind was still clear. She ended up chatting with him, listening to the stories behind the crooked nose and the empty socket sealed up by the taut purplish eyelid. Wondering what or when exactly in this rambling tale of failures and losses and mindless violence had been the point of no return from which it had become impossible to keep on hoping and fighting. Or had there even been such a point? And what kept him from jumping into the Seine to end it all for good.

Then a genteel-looking young man came up to tell the homeless guy about a nearby charity run by nuns who could provide him with warm food, and even clothes if he needed any. The bum chuckled, shaking his head, accusing nuns in general of trying to get him on the wagon. What's the point of lying, he confessed, the first thing he would get when he had collected enough money was some alcohol. He simply couldn't survive without the stupor—not his exact terms but close enough.

Two trains had gone by and she really had to get on the next one. She gave him a feeble goodbye smile before turning away. "*Allez,*" he smiled back, "you don't have to look so sad, it's my life, not yours." Or something sounding just as shockingly lucid and resigned.

She usually ignores beggars. Doesn't feel guilty about her attitude as she doesn't feel she's ever being judgmental about the individuals themselves. But their begging unnerves her. It is sometimes so damn hard to get up in the morning and move on to the next day, the next job to put some food on your plate; hard not to feel like giving up the struggle yourself. So you walk past them who have given up and sit or sprawl motionless on the sidewalk, moving on, careful not to let their eyes meet yours.

Because she's not even sure what it is that keeps her moving these days, these idle pointless days now that her last silly illusion has burst into thin air. What more would it take for her to become a bag lady herself, she wonders. She clings to the merciful routine of daily tasks that give some semblance of structure to her small sorry existence. They are a true blessing as they keep her on some sort of track at least.

Still, sometimes an old familiar anguish creeps back to sap her energy, the strange nauseous sensation of having strayed into another dimension lurking right inside this world, from which she can still see and hear and feel with fully functioning senses the actual world around her, but is insidiously moved to wonder if she is truly part of it, if she is fully sentient and awake to it. Like some usually undetectable tear in the fabric of things that will suddenly open up into an invisible gap that is not substantially there, she knows, she's not delirious, but it feels so tangible, so tangibly gaping there, threatening to engulf her sanity, that her pulse starts racing, panic settles in, the old fight-and-flight reflex; only there is nothing to fight against and nowhere to fly from, or to, and she is left stranded on this alien side of reality, looking around with alien eyes, wanting frantically to be back *in* where her body *actually is.*

And she will often find herself listening in for the incipient signs of yet another nauseous spell, instinctively bracing herself.

But then a spark out of a trifling detail or an insignificant occurrence manages to light up a moment, and lightens her mood, and she has no idea why either.

Or then again she finds herself obsessing compulsively over some vivid image she can't shake off her mind that crystallizes a fluid emotion she can't put her finger on. How sickly emotional, she realizes, but there it is, gnawing at her.

Until another replaces it. Or her emotions are suddenly uplifted by yet another transient, ungraspable shade of light.

Or not.

· • • ● • ● • • ·

"But it really seems like you've given up, Anne."

Frankie is being condescending and that is really infuriating. Anne lashes out: "*You*'re the one who gave up. Come on, isn't that the life of quiet desperation we had vowed to keep out of? Manager of a language institute, is that what you completed your Master's for?"

"Well, I had to make some choices at some point. I chose to follow Pierre and so here I am, dealing with the consequences, that's all." She doesn't raise her voice, or flinch in any perceptible way. "Are you sure you're not just dreaming your life away in this tiny little *chambre de bonne* though?" she insists, gesturing around the small attic room.

"But can't you see, Frankie? I don't even understand what it is I'm not supposed to give up on. I can't have that faith or whatever it is that keeps you buoyant and eager to make something of your life."

"So what's your alternative? Drift whichever way until death claims you?"

"Right, be a winner or a loser. What else could you possibly be, right? Well, I'm not even a *tryer*, for Christ's sake."

"You told me you had been married, so obviously you *tried* at some point. Why didn't you go all the way and make kids? Believe me, they cure you of any self-centered indulgence in existential angst."

Could that be her irritation filtering through at last?

"You're right, actually, I tried—" Anne starts replying, breaking off in mid-sentence, her voice suspended on its rising tone for a fraction of a second.

So here it comes then, emerging suddenly out of the choppy surface of their silly argument. Yet does she really want to tell her full story to this woman she barely knows anymore and keeps tugging at her heartstrings with a vengeance?

"I even got pregnant, to tell you the whole truth, but I miscarried."

There, she said it. She lets Frankie fumble for some appropriate answer, then decides to let it all out before the impulse dries up: "It was a stillbirth, actually. The baby's heart just stopped beating one day, a few weeks before he was due. There was no clear cause the doctors could identify."

"I'm so sorry. I had no idea."

"Even after the ultrasound that confirmed it, I couldn't register. Even after I was induced. It was such a shock, I only had a few weeks to go—"

"It happens sometimes, unfortunately."

But Frankie can't let it go so fast. Because letting go is definitely not part of Frankie's mental make-up, she who prides herself on keeping positive and practical no matter what. "Didn't you give it another chance?" she can't refrain from asking, her voice awkwardly soft still.

"That's exactly what everybody advised me to do. After they felt I'd had enough time to recover, of course. But the truth is, deep down I could relate to the baby's choice not to be born after all."

"Come on Anne," Frankie cuts her off, unable to repress some hint of irritation in her soft sympathetic voice. "You know it wasn't the fetus's choice to die, and hurt you."

"I don't mean like it was a rational choice, of course. Just a lack of natural drive, you know, that common urge in all living beings,

I guess. He clearly didn't have enough of it pushing him to keep growing."

"I'm so sorry," Frankie whispers again.

"It's all right. It's an old story now, but it took me a while—"

A while to do what, she asks herself inwardly. *Get closure?* She clearly hasn't been able to yet, after all this time. But how can she explain it to her friend?

"I don't know if I can even put it into words. My child died inside my womb and I actually gave birth to a dead fetus, and that's no metaphor, Frankie: I was made to deliver that tiny little dead boy. My breasts even started lactating after it was all over."

But how can she express it without sounding too morbidly emotional?

"It was not just the pain never to get to hold that little boy I was lactating for, you see. It was, like his refusal to be born that really shook me."

This time Frankie refrains from correcting her and extends her hand instead.

"My husband couldn't relate to my pain. At all. He didn't really feel there was anybody to mourn. I don't blame him, the baby didn't exist enough for him yet, even if we had already given him a name. In fact, Will wanted to try again almost immediately. After all, the nursery was ready, the baby names chosen, the savings account opened, why wait? The guy's very much into perseverance too."

Frankie smiles a lukewarm version of her lopsided smile.

"I'm not making fun, mind you," Anne continues. Her hand frees itself from Frankie's hold and starts flitting about, trying to help shape her emotions into some intelligible pattern: "But see, the baby left a void inside my body. Like some sort of resonance chamber I still can't stop listening in to. "

"All this time you've been living in a chronic state of depression, Anne," Frankie concludes.

"Have I? But then, tell me Frankie, who isn't?" Because aren't we all of us weighed down by the same entropic pull towards decay and and back to dust, what else is there in the end anyway but dust, literally, the actual dust of stars in every atom of matter. "Or tell me what it is that keeps people so busy and focused. Putting all their energy into building their lives and careers, marriages, homes, all the things people do in a lifetime."

"That's precisely what life is all about," Frankie replies. "To build and plan the best you can. Dealing with the real world the way it is."

"But what's so real about all this in the end?"

"Come on Anne, the real world is simply what you have to come to terms with, one way or another, so you can survive in it."

But Anne is shaking her head, stubbornly. "I'll tell you what felt the most real to me that warm spring afternoon when my labor was induced, after it was all over and I was alone recovering in my hospital room: the breeze that kept moving the blind through the open window, sucking it in and out, like a gentle metallic singsong. That breath of fresh air was the only moving entity in the empty room, so gentle and playful, blowing through my confusion and pain. Everything was so mixed up all of a sudden, so chaotic, and it was all so vivid and intense, beyond any words I can find—"

She pauses in the middle of her sentence, heart racing, catches herself half listening in for the familiar nauseous signs.

"Everything's so tangled up, living, growing, decaying, dying, that's our true natural environment, the only *real* I can truly trust. Desire and joy all mixed up with pain and loss. What could be more realistic than to listen in to all of this fluid ambivalence and ride the mood swings?"

Frankie stares at her, refraining from saying anything this time, only enfolding her friend's hand again in a firm grip. What sense is she even supposed to make of this nihilistic mumbo jumbo?

"What if you're just, like, shell shocked, still?" She figures. "You could suffer from PTSD because of what you've been through. I mean, how could it not be unbearable to give birth to *death*, literally, as you said? A stillborn baby, that's too much of a paradox to handle, too much to cope with, emotionally and *existentially*."

"But why does it have to be so pathological, Frankie? If anything, my painful experience seems to have stimulated my instinct for survival, don't you see? I chose to remain alive in all this confusion, didn't I?"

"But did you?" Frankie blurts out. "I mean, what if you're just kidding yourself? What if you're still in mourning and can't come out of it? And you can't stop lingering in some sort of limbo between life and death?"

"Can we cut out the psych 101 crap, Frankie, already? I want nothing more than to be healthy and sane, believe you me, that's my whole point. My only ambition, in fact. Only, I want to tune *in* for real."

"Oh I see, because the rest of us are just clueless zombies," Frankie allows herself to jeer. "Oh yes, I get it now, it reminds me of, who was it? Lennon, was it? life is what happens when we're too busy making plans, right?"

Anne lets a pause disperse all the static crackling between them.

"Is that what you think I'm saying, Frankie?" she replies in a subdued voice. "All I'm saying is that what seems to be right for you can't work for me, simple as that. So call me a misfit, suits me fine. Better be an accomplished one, then, I guess. Which is why I've decided to keep the logistics of my existence down to the basics."

She realizes her shy smile is an appeal for leniency.

"Comfortable enough though, I must admit, because it's not like I'm claiming to be a monk or a believer in any creed. I am creedless, but so what? Can't there be such a thing as an agnostic contemplative?"

She lets out a strained little laugh. Frankie shrugs, noncommittal.

Anne sobers up. "Look, I'm definitely the clueless one here, I'm not denying it, believe me. Because the truth is, right when I thought I had given up on all illusions I started writing this novel, which turned out to be just another lame construction. Just a self-delusional attempt at order and coherence. It turned out so trite and melodramatic anyway. I obviously can't find the words, so I must let go of that too."

But then why won't all these words stop gushing, she wonders, embarrassed at her own inconsistency, and at the silly tears misting her eyes. Frankie's face is now a hazy moon in the mellow evening sunlight slanting through the skylight, and her stylish grey linen suit is shimmering like blue silk.

She has vowed not to indulge in the self-pitying pathos anymore, true, but this is a different mood, yes, quietly lucid, sad maybe, but soft and soothing. Maybe it's only this in the end, that at times, in a fluke light effect, grey can soften itself into blue.

FIVE

"SO HOW DID IT go this time?"

"Not too bad, considering."

The truth is, the whole business keeps getting more comical every time and he is not sure he is any mood just now to brief Anne on the latest episode. The hint of a smile is already curling up one corner of her mouth. Why add any more fuel to her mirth?

But then, why not? She helps him get a lighter angle on things, that's always good. She sure has a knack of putting things in the quirkiest perspective imaginable.

They're sitting on the sidewalk terrace of their favorite café, enjoying the cooler sunrays at the end of another hot blazing day. Only the curve of her lips reveal anything about her take on his story as the sardonic glint of her eyes is hidden behind her opaque shades. She seems to be taking things pretty cool and easy these days. Pretty laidback. Is she seeing whatshisname again, he wonders. Getting laid at any rate. Not that she tells him much any more.

"Well, I got to meet Bérengère's big brother, Bertrand. A really nice guy in fact. Just back from one of those French islands in the Pacific where he worked for a couple years. He's in the medical field too, but doing research I think. Anyway, he is married. So, guess what?"

"What?"

"I spent the whole weekend hanging on the wife's every word to try and figure out how *she* was calling the parents."

"Talk about an obsession."

"Yeah well, it got me nowhere anyhow. Can you believe the lady didn't address those folks in any distinct way the whole time we were there?"

"What? She's a mute?"

She's got the cutest yet most irritating smirk on her lips now. He knows he's about to make it blossom into a broad toothy smile, but what the hell.

"Hell no, the woman is a talker all right. In fact, she never stops talking, and man, do they love her too. She goes on and on and they can't get enough of it. But see, the way she does it, it's so fucking mindboggling: I never once heard her call them *Maman* and *Papa*, or *Mamie* and *Papy* like her kid, or even Jacques and Hélène; or say *tu*, or *vous*, or *sa mighty grand majesté* or whatever, for crying out loud. And yet she can't seem to stop talking to them, you know, like (straining his voice into a high-pitched imitation of the woman's simpering) '*Chéri, les roses de ton père sont magnifiques*' or 'Lola, or Lila, that's their little kid—*adore les tartelettes de sa grand-mère, n'est-ce pas ma chérie?*' "

"She seems like a natural at this game."

"And what game could that be, may I ask? Don't you think it's about time somebody let me in on the fucking rules here?"

She's laughing of course, and he glimpses the brightness of his own teeth flickering in her lenses.

"Maybe the only rule is that you're *it* no matter what."

She's obviously proud of her bold assumption.

"What the hell are you talking about?"

"See, as soon as you're not around she starts acting normal with them, calling them *tu* or *vous* or whatever it is they've agreed she should call them. But then, when you're there too she reverts back to her evasiveness, just to annoy you."

He stares at her opaque shades, nodding and laughing at his own tiny twin reflections in disbelief.

"You know, the craziest part of this is, I'm not even sure it can be totally ruled out. I'm telling you, those tricksters are not above pulling something like this on me, just for the fun of it."

"Well, look at it this way: you finally got an answer to your obsessive questioning, didn't you? Talk to them through Bérengère and then start getting her pregnant to add more pawns to your game. Then you can start playing in the major league too."

"Right!" he nods with thoughtful deliberation, smiling. "But what if I'm *it* with the kids too? My own flesh and blood? What then?"

"You're marrying into a foreign family, Matt."

"A fucking terra incognita you mean."

"You'll do just fine. Don't fret so much."

And she gives him a nice, comforting smile. What does she care anyway?

SIX

W HEN THE TAXI DROPS her off in front of the building whose address she had carefully penciled on a piece of paper, it is raining even harder than it was back at the airport. She steps onto the wet sidewalk, picks up her luggage from the curb on which the driver has left it and hurries across the avenue to take shelter under the awning of a brasserie. Number 152, that's the big door right there. Once inside, she'll have to find her way to the apartment—the attic room rather, if she remembers correctly from the few messages over the last eighteen months. There may be one of those Parisian caretakers stationed in a lodge inside, since this definitely looks like a typical Parisian building.

All right then, no point in waiting any longer, let's get it over with. Anne won't be too happy with the surprise. But what else could be done in the end, she's stopped answering letters and emails entirely these last few weeks.

As could be expexted though, the big door is locked. There is a digital keypad and of course she doesn't know the code. She rolls her suitcase back across the avenue and resumes her position under the awning, her carry-on bag tightly held against her, shivering and miserable. Wondering if she shouldn't just get settled in her hotel first, freshen up and rest a bit. But then, as if by magic, the *concierge* she had been expecting to meet inside comes out to retrieve the green rollout trash cans taken out earlier for the garbage collection.

Friendly chatty Madame Pereira Gonçalves greets the American lady with her usual cheerful exuberance: *"Ah, mais alors vous êtes la maman d'Anne ! Mais oui elle est là, venez, venez !"* and she pushes the big heavy door open, forgetting all about the trash cans to grab the suitcase and show the visitor into the lobby, an excited flow of words bubbling out of her laughing mouth all the while.

Next to the glass door of the lodge, opposite the red-carpeted staircase and the old-style narrow elevator shaft, a short corridor leads to a steep spiral staircase. The warm concierge holds the lady's arm and points up at the ceiling: *"C'est tout là-haut !"* She gestures towards the darkly lit corridor, opens her left hand and holds up her right thumb beside it to clarify her point: *"C'est au sixième étage, tout en haut."* She now points at the suitcase, gesturing towards her lodge: *"Mais vous pouvez laisser vos bagages dans ma loge pour le moment."* Anne's mother nods evasively, trying to take everything in. Is there really no elevator to go all the way to the sixth floor? Her dismay is so palpable the concierge pulls her gently into the front room of her lodge. *"Venez, venez, j'ai une idée, je vais appeler Anne sur son portable, elle descendra."* She reaches for the phone on a corner shelf, punches in a number from a list neatly thumbtacked to the wall above the receiver. Beaming a broad happy smile as soon as she hears the voice at the other end of the line: *"Anne, descends vite, il y a une surprise pour toi ici."* The visitor is still hesitating in the doorway.

• • • • • • • • • •

When Anne finally comes down, she doesn't see right away the uncomfortable lady sitting there in the corner seat with a cup of coffee in her trembling fingers, poignantly foreign and out of place. She peeps in expectantly through the glass door and greets Madame Pereira Gonçalves cheerfully before her eyes light on the visitor, and the smile freezes on her face. Her mother stares back anxiously, securing the cup and saucer on the table next to her. "I'm really sorry to barge in on you like this, honey." Then standing up, her eyes filling with tears, waiting for her daughter to step in and hug her at last. "It's been so long, Annie. You've shut us all out of your life for much too long."

When Madame Pereira Gonçalves had called to announce a surprise, she expected a big bunch of flowers as a follow up on another night of make up sex in a complicated on and off realtionship, and she was bracing herself for the *concierge*'s motherly teasing. But here was her actual mother in the flesh. Older and thinner than the familiar picture stored in her memory along with the repressed guilt. Doesn't the mistreated past always end up knocking on your door when you least expect it?

Anne couldn't possibly take her mother up to her nest, or cell, let her see the stark austerity of it, the squat toilet in the grimy corridor. Up six flights of stairs anyway, to what would actually be called the seventh floor in an American building. So they went to the brasserie for breakfast, before taking a taxi to the hotel.

Her mother brought her up to date on all the family news. Anne listened dutifully, nodding and smiling, thankful for the natural pauses in the conversation eating allowed. Then she answered questions about the details of her life in Paris. Until the crucial one finally came up, the one her mother had flown all this way to ask her.

"Don't you think it's time to come back to where you belong, honey? Not to your marriage of course," she hastened to clarify, "I understand that this is all over. But your father and I could help you put all this behind you and get back on track. Even go back to college, if you wanted to finish your degree." She paused and touched her daughter's cheek with her trembling fingers. "Aren't you getting tired of all this, Anne?"

Yes, she is tired, more than she will admit to herself in her stubborn refusal to face her options. But what if she goes back only to get bogged down again? Can she risk losing the freedom she has found here, in this intimate place far away from home?

Or maybe go back to college indeed, to her unfinished business there, and work on something substantial enough to release her pent-up energy. Why not, say, the relevance of Thoreau's legacy at the dawn of the 21st century? Instead of hiding away in her sad pretense of a cabin with its blind rectangular eye cut out of the slanting roof, her little comfy cocoon, like a stubborn recluse stuck in her morbid unwillingness (wasn't Frankie right in the end?) to embrace either life or death. Or even cut the self-indulgent crap altogether, go back home to get a decent job, maybe join an organization fighting to save life on this precious blue planet before it is too late?

Such a simple choice to make in the end.

She's no spring chicken anymore, her vistas have shrunk, but why couldn't she rekindle in herself the simple natural zest for living she once had, as a small child at least, as the happy carefree little girl she can remember being ages ago; or the newborn she can't remember, who gasped for her first breath of air after tearing herself out of the body of this now tired and frail woman imploring her to get back to where she belongs.

SEVEN

THEIR LAST *APÉRITIF* TOGETHER at the café and it is taking an unpleasant turn. She wishes she had broken it to him before, instead of point-blank like this.

"I'm really sorry Matt, but I'm scheduled to leave in two weeks."

"What's the big rush all of a sudden? You're my best friend here, you know that. I need you with me that day. I depend on you to be by my side."

She shakes her head, half suppressing a smirk. "Aren't you being a little excessive here, sweetheart? Where do you think exactly I'd be standing in the picture? The only person you depend on to be by your side is the one about to become your lawfully wedded wife. I'm very replaceable, believe you me."

He is so tense and scared it's almost comical. Where's the cool easy-go-funky Matt hiding in this possessed body?

"Come on Anne, I need you, you know that. Nobody but my mother will be coming," he explodes, spluttering his frustration through his nasal congestion, his first rhinitis of the rainy fall. "I'll have only a few friends of my own there, and if *you*'re not there I'm gonna feel like a mere extra at my own wedding."

She's both moved and annoyed by his distress. Why is he making things so much more uncomfortable than they have to be?

"Matt, I love you like the little brother I never had, I swear, but now we have to go our separate ways, can't you see?

"But what's a few more weeks here, for crying out loud? Then you'll have the rest of your life to be on your own separate way." He pulls his visor lower over his eyes but can't mute the crack in his voice.

"The fact is, my mother made sure I had booked my flight back before she took off."

"Can't you do that for me, postpone your departure date for just a few weeks? Come on, what difference would that make in the big scheme?"

Funny how their affection for each other has never been awkwardly ambiguous or marred by any frivolous flirting. She'll miss him so much, it suddenly hits her. And catches herself fighting the silly urge to hug him in spite of his nasty cold. Again she tries to explain, calmly, soothingly: "I'm truly sorry if it feels to you like I'm being a jerk. But I wish you would understand how hard it was to make that decision to leave in the first place. I'm afraid of my own impulses if I change anything in the plan as it stands."

He shakes his head, lips pursed. Then sighs resignedly. "I don't know what's wrong with me, Anne. Look at the sniveling sop I'm turning into, what a disgrace." Blowing his nose plangently. "And what do I expect them to do to me at my own wedding anyway?"

"I don't think French weddings are so very different from the American thing," she concurs in a reassuring big-sisterly kind of tone. "I don't think they're going to require any sort of exotic ritual feat involving any self-maiming on your part. A wedding, even French, is not a rite of initiation, now is it?"

He finally flashes at her his old urchin smile, and pushes back his cap to scratch his forehead.

"Well, in all honesty, it does feel a bit like a rite of initiation. I mean, getting married is so grown up. What if I'm still in the last stage of my final growth spurt?"

He lets out a little chuckle before looking intently into her eyes, dead serious now, as if daring her to laugh at him: "I love Bérengère like I've never loved any woman before, I'm sure I want her to be my wife," he reminds himself emphatically, "and I can't wait to put that ring on her finger in front of all these people so they can start taking me seriously."

"That's the right attitude, little bro. Show'em."

He shrugs, toying with his empty glass. "It's just that now you're leaving and I'm getting married, and everything's changing so fast, it's all so radical."

"You just have to go with the flow. You're a good swimmer, aren't you?"

He still looks at her with the same intensity.

"Maybe if I had looked at your computer more thoroughly that day, and if I had found your novel where it was hiding right there on the screen, you'd still be writing it and wouldn't even think of leaving now."

"Is that what you're thinking? Sweetheart, losing that novel was the best thing that could happen to me, honestly."

"Maybe so, but how can you be so sure?" he muses, fingering his glass distractedly. "Anyway, I like it when you call me sweetheart in this new non sarcastic way," he smiles, sliding the glass back on the table. "Cause it wasn't sarcastic, right? I'm not always sure how to take things with you."

They're grinning at each other as if sizing each other up playfully, appraising the tightness of their bond.

"Anyway", he says, breaking the intimate moment. "I need a refill to help me get a better perspective on all those major changes in my life. Want another one too? My treat again, since you're the one leaving, I guess."

EIGHT

S HE IS BUSY FILLING up the last boxes with leftover things, knicknacks and books to be given away, a mass of things to get rid of before she can fly away, light and free.

Luc shows up at the open door, checks out the emptying room silently.

"The *concierge* told me you were leaving tomorrow," he finally says, giving her an angry glare that she tries to ignore while sorting through her pile of books.

"In two days actually."

She can't even make herself look up straight at him standing there in the doorway, leaning against the doorjamb, shaking his head ever so slightly at the far edge of her visual field.

"So that's why you just don't return my calls."

He squats down next to her, setting his hands square on the pile of books, his face level with hers so she can't keep averting her eyes. "Why *now* Anne?"

"Because it's time to get back and figure out what I'm going to do with the rest of my life, don't you think? I can't keep on hiding like this for ever, can I?"

"Just like that, then—" Shaking his head again in that unnerving tic of his.

She wants to keep her voice low and unemotional, keep things under control. This is precisely what she's been trying so hard to avoid, the clumsy explanations.

"Come on, you knew I was planning on leaving some day soon."

"But I hoped you'd reconsider." And then, angry again: "What are you running away from anyway?"

"Not *away! Back!* You knew that," she snaps at him, pushing his limp hands off the pile of books. And back she goes to boxing the books. Sensing her determination almost about to flinch, quite frankly. But she won't allow him to do that to her, no way, not now that she's finally resolved on a sensible course of action.

He sits down, pushing the boxes aside, cross-legged right in front of her. His half-buttoned shirt gaping over a sizeable triangle of bare skin her attention is magnetically drawn to, just as she can't help being stirred by his familiar eau de toilette. He takes her face in his hands. "You could stay for *me*."

"And how fair would that be?" she snarls, breaking loose. "Am I asking you to come to the States with me?"

"What could I be doing in the States?" he snarls back. "I have a good job here, I can't just leave like that."

"Well then, what would I be doing here, besides continuing my ridiculous little clandestine life?"

Again he grabs her face, locking his eyes on hers. "You chose the secrecy, Anne. It doesn't have to be this way." He is begging more than pressuring now, dabbing the tears of rage from her cheeks. "Just give us a chance, that's all I'm asking."

And now she can't stop herself from shivering, her tense body relaxing, releasing itself from the grip of her rage; rising to this urgent pull, the ebb and flow of his breath, of her own breath swelling in sync.

The tempo speeds up and she slides into it, she doesn't miss a beat, swept off, weightless. Lifted off high above her stubborn fears, gliding away, deaf to the sardonic laugh under her flesh, the bony sneer under the kissing lips. Listening in to the urgent question pulsing through the fingers caressing her skin: do you even know where you really want to belong?

NINE

THE MORNING HAS BEEN spent drawing up the guest list for the wedding, which will be a rather small, quiet affair, Bérengère's parents promised. They have been courteously inquiring if he is sure no one else will be coming on his side of the family. Maybe his half-sister, he answers, who'd love to, but can't promise for sure yet, as she would have to obtain an exceptional leave of absence from her boss at a time when business is brisk. Anyhow, the newlyweds will put off the honeymoon until next summer so he can introduce his bride to his relatives in Cleveland. They listen to him, very considerate. Well, they'll be delighted to welcome his mother in their home for as long as she wants to stay in France, they assure him warmly. Even Hélène is definitely mellowing to him, as if she's coming to grip with the fact that he will soon be her son-in-law, an undisputable and fully legitimate member of her family. She's even stopped bitching on and on about the silly date her wacky daughter came up with all by herself after much astrological rumination it seems, November of all months, and what was the rush *vraiment*? Matt is starting to relax.

After lunch they'll visit a local gourmet inn to order the half dozen course wedding feast with matching wines. It is all very impressive, all this ceremonious planning for the big event, and he is acting his part with as much dignity as he can summon up. Anyway, they'll pay for everything so that's a huge weight off his shoulders right there. Might as well try and enjoy it. His big day, they keep telling him excitedly, and they seem so convinced they can't be totally off base, he figures. How could he go terribly wrong during the proceedings anyway? It should be simple enough. These people love to party and have impeccable taste in everything, you can grant them that much. Better let them make the crucial decisions by themselves, he'll just show up when his presence is required. His contribution, besides starring as the male lead in the cast, will be to take the photographs himself, with an assistant for the group pictures in which he'll have to appear, and of course for those of the bride and groom.

Bérengère comes out into the garden to lay the table in the shade of an old lime tree. She is resplendent, getting more so every day it seems, and whatever cold feet he might be close to having sometimes, she just fixes instantaneously with her light breezy ways, whirling all around him so his head keeps spinning. He's so besotted he finds himself acting increasingly corny around her. She doesn't seem to mind, or notice for that matter.

Lunch today is BBQ, Matt style, with potato salad and coleslaw that he made himself too. He has gone up a notch in their esteem, he can tell, and that's always good, and if it's all it takes—

And until he has finally figured out the *tu/vous* situation, he's been playing it safe thanks to Bertrand's wife's nifty strategy, using Bérengère as a relay station, sort of, in his addresses to her parents. He's become remarkably deft at this.

• • • • • • • • • •

The innkeeper is a big burly fellow with a gruff kind of joviality and a plump good-hearted wife. They don't seem to belong to the same social circle as the Beaufort folks, but they all seem to get along fantastically. Maybe a tad too fantastically, as it will soon turn out.

"*Alors Bérengère*, he's the right one this time, *tu es sûre?*" Monsieur Berteau jabs as soon as the proper introductions have been made with the right amount of handshakes (men to men) and appropriate cheek-kissing (all the other combinations), two on either side around here, as they keep reminding him, and even each other occasionally, whenever they go through the little ritual.

"*Ah non Jean-Paul, ne commence pas,*" his wife cries out, giggling as she embraces Bérengère in a bosomy hug." Don't mind him, *ma poulette*, he's just a doddering old fool and he's sure not getting any better as the years go by."

Even *Maman* is smiling gracefully without the slightest trace of irritation distorting her fine features.

"Jean-Paul is the mayor of our little town," Jacques explains to Matt. "He'll be performing the ceremony at the *mairie*, so we don't want to upset him and that's why we're using his inn, never mind the cost."

They all laugh to ascertain it was meant as a harmless joke. Matt nods and smiles for lack of anything intelligent-sounding to reply.

"Does he speak adequate French?" blunt Jean- Paul now asks." We sure want the poor fellow to understand what's going to happen to him, right?" he booms, laughing his jolly boisterous laugh.

"No need to worry, he's perfectly fluent," Jacques assures his buddy, "Not much of an accent even."

"Barely detectable," Hélène concurs with her odd little lip-pursing smile.

"So what does he do for a living? You can't live on love and fresh water alone, *n'est-ce pas?*" the florid innkeeper carries on. "You've got to work, even with a beautiful wife like that keeping you busy and sleepless at night."

"*Enfin Jean-Paul, voyons!*" the wife scolds again, giggling again, and again embracing Bérengère in a smothering hug.

"*Allons bon, tu exagères Jean-Paul,*" Jacques exclaims with only half-pretend indignation, stealing an uncertain glance at his wife.

"Matt teaches English," Bérengère hastens to reply to steer the jolly jester away from the slippery sass.

"Give Matt a chance to speak, *ma chérie,*" Hélène cuts in, looking encouragingly at Matt.

"I work for a language institute in Paris."

"The pay's not bad," Jacques points out. "He's doing pretty well for himself. And he's also a very good photographer, isn't he?"

"*C'est vrai,* that's my real vocation, only a hobby right now."

"Who knows, if he's got talent," Madame Berteau says, looking at him encouragingly.

"He's actually very talented!" Bérengère answers proudly.

"Let Matt express himself, my dear," Jacques says gently, looking at him encouragingly.

"Well, I used to work for a news magazine in the US, but—"

"Why did he leave, then? Did he get tired of living there? I know I would," monsieur Berteau says.

"What do you know about America?" Jacques chuckles. "*Tu exagères toujours.*"

"*C'est vrai, vous exagérez Jean-Paul,* you've been there only once, on a very short holiday!" Hélène protests.

"Everything's too big over there: big cars, big houses, big portions at restaurants, big women. I like my small Renault and my small woman just fine, *moi.*"

"*Enfin Jean-Paul*, because of you Matt's going to tell everybody there that the French are chauvinists," the wife, who's not all that small actually, chides again, without indulging in a simultaneous fit of giggling this time.

"Yeah well, why did he come all the way here to steal one of our most beautiful girls, then?"

"*Enfin Jean-Paul, vraiment vous exagérez!* » Héléne retorts with audible displeasure, and now her features are starting to show unmistakable signs of annoyance.

"Matt mustn't mind him," Madame Berteau laughs. "*Vous savez bien, Hélène,* this man doesn't mean half of what he says. He can't be taken seriously."

"I'm sure he realizes I'm just a jolly old fool, doesn't he, Bérengère?"

"I don't know, ask him!"

Everybody laughs to ascertain Bérengère's terse reply was just another harmless joke.

Matt forces a chuckle out. What about the fucking menu, he can't help wondering. When does this become part of the goofy conversation?

Jean-Paul winks at him. "He's probably ready to get down to business, isn't he?"

Fuck, is the man a polyglot mind reader on top of a blundering jokester?

"I don't suppose he's much of a connoisseur of French cuisine, so you'll have to do the translating and describing, Bérengère,"

Madame Berteau says, taking Hélène's arm to lead the way to the back office from which she manages the family business. "*Alors*, you prefer fish for the first course, *vous êtes sûre* ?"

"The children like it better that way. Matt doesn't care much for *charcuterie.*"

They have all crowded into the small room and she takes some laminated sheets of paper out of a drawer.

"What about our *magret de canard sauce aux cèpes* for the first main course? *Qu'en penses-tu Bérengère, toi?*"

"Great!"

"*Canard* is duck, right?" Matt verifies in English.

"Yes, with some mushroom sauce, why?" she whispers back.

"I don't know, my mother might find it a little too exotic for her taste."

"You can't change that without hurting their feelings," Bérengère whispers hurriedly. "It's a specialty in this inn. Just tell her it's chicken, she'll love it."

He flashes his charm smile at her. Still never fails to marvel at her quirky instinct for extraspeed crisis management.

Jean-Paul is staring at them with a naughty glint in his eyes. "*Dites donc* love birds, leave the *coquin* talk for the wedding night and help us figure this thing out, *d'accord?*"

Jacques chuckles sotto voce: "*Vraiment Jean-Paul, tu exagères,* you shouldn't talk like this in front of the ladies."

But the ladies are oblivious to the husbands' coarsening mood as they are now concentrating on a catalog of menu prototypes that Madame Berteau has borrowed from the local printer to help her friends save time.

"Maybe you should let Bérengère choose the menu herself. She will probably keep it as a souvenir in her photo album, won't you, *ma poulette?*"

"*Vous avez raison, Aline.*" And so Bérengère is pulled into the women's group while the men go to the bar counter to get drinks.

"I'm going to let Matt taste the pomerol that will honor his wedding day," Jean-Paul announces with uncharacteristic discretion.

Matt takes the glass that is handed to him, glowing ruby red in the dim electric light, and takes a dainty sip.

"Does he like it?" Jean-Paul asks, eagerly waiting for his reaction.

Matt hums in appreciation.

"I guess Coca Cola hasn't totally numbed his taste buds after all!"

Matt takes another sip and hums again with more determination.

"He seems to have the right palate for quality wine. Not so bad, *ton beau-fils*, Jacques." Jean-Paul pokes at Matt's shoulder with the bottle and pours some more wine into his half emptied glass.

"Now let's keep this low key, *les gars*," he whispers conspiratorially. "If the wife learns that I have opened another bottle of pomerol just for the fun of it, I won't hear the end of this. This is one of the best vintages, does he realize it?" he winks at Matt.

"Of course he does, he is not such an uncouth lout, *n'est-ce pas* Matt?" Jacques whispers back with subdued mirth.

"Of course he's not!" agrees Matt, humming again to prove he definitely is not, for all his unfortunate Americanness.

As the ladies' footsteps are heard coming their way, the bottle swiftly vanishes under the counter.

"What are you men up to?" Aline half scolds half giggles. "Letting us work out all the serious business by ourselves as usual." Then turning to Matt: "Maybe he should go to the bakery along with Bérengère and Hélène to choose the *pièce montée.*"

"The wedding cake," Bérengère explains to her fiancé's quizzical stare.

"But why don't you women leave him alone? What does he care what the *pièce montée* will look like?" Jean-Paul winks at Matt. "Let him stay here with us so we can finish our serious political discussion."

"*Oh tu exagères*, we all know what you men are up to," Madame Berteau exclaims. "So, does he want to come with us or stay with the men?" she asks Matt good-humoredly.

"*C'est vous qui exagérez maintenant, Aline*, Jacques chortles. What do you mean, stay with the men, like he's a poodle or something, *vraiment!*"

"Of course he's staying!" Jean-Paul booms out laughing. "*Bon sang*, the poor fellow has probably no idea what the *pièce montée* should look like, *n'est-ce pas?*"

"Not really," Matt says, feeling his head spin a little. "He's never been to a French wedding before, let alone his own!"

The truth is, he's not sure how long he'll be able to remain in his neat upright position, propped against the wall perpendicular to the bar. Lunch has been washed down with a great Saint-Emilion, on top of the preliminary whisky, and finally a local liqueur as a coda.

Jean-Paul laughs even louder, poking Matt on the shoulder with his empty glass. "You'll have to promise to bring your son-in-law around anytime he is in town, Jacques. There are so many political things to discuss around here."

Bérengère shakes her head in exasperation and follows the two older ladies out of the large banquet room. As soon as the door of the inn is heard chiming shut, Jean-Paul chooses another bottle from the shelf behind him. "Listen, you've got to taste that coteau-du-layon, Jacques, it would be perfect for the *foie gras* at the *apéritif, tu vas voir.*"

He is still whispering although the disturbing factor is gone. He shoots another gleeful conspiratorial wink at his guests and takes clean glasses for the new bottle. "I am in contact with this excellent wine grower who still works the old traditional way and *bon sang*, you can taste the difference."

The amber-colored liqueur gleams enticingly in the subdued light. Matt is wondering how much longer this crash course in prestige wine tasting is going to last, though. He wouldn't like to disappoint his host, but he sure is starting to feel seriously dizzy.

"That's what you call Little Lord Jesus in his velvet breeches, it goes so smooth down your throat," Jacques winks, in sync with his buddy Jean-Paul, whose every facial tic he now seems to duplicate.

Matt nods politely. He might have misheard anyway. Still, shouldn't these old guys take their reverence a little more seriously, just in case? Maybe their old village priest should remember to mention a few words about God's Wrath in his sermons, occasionally. Instead of rushing his flock through mass to get them all out of his church as soon as possible. Even forgot to give them all communion once. Matt chuckles drunkenly, shifting unsteadily on his feet, holding on to the bar. The senile old priest forgot to feed his parishioners the body of Christ once, or so the story goes, impatient that he was to get back to the presbytery for his Sunday roast. So what, mishaps happen, ha ha! Nobody minded the extra short service anyway. Matt can't stop the chuckling now, reminiscing privately the funny story he's been told several times (since of course that's the country priest who's supposed to marry them). These lucky people are on such friendly terms with their Holy Trinity, all venial sinners that they are. Such a baroque world of strange old traditions.

Meanwhile, Jean-Paul has disappeared into the cellar somewhere below the building.

"Isn't he a nice man, Jean-Paul?"

"He seems to be very much into exaggerating," Matt slurs incoherently.

"Does he?" Jacques chuckles. "Well, he knows how to live, this man. He should go easy on the liquor, sure, but, well, he grew up on a vineyard around here, good wine is his passion. Of course it might be argued that he takes his wine tasting with a little too much zeal, but one shouldn't hold it against him, such a nice man."

The doctor raises his glass and peers through the rest of the golden liquid.

"One has to understand, we've known the Berteaus for thirty years. After he was elected mayor, the very first marriage he performed was Bertrand and Sophie's, and quite naturally, the wedding reception took place here. And then three years ago Jean-Paul had prostate cancer. I had retired by then but I had been the family's physician for all these years so, naturally, I still made frequent calls on him, as a friend, and that's how we became closer."

"Close enough to be on a *tu* basis."

"That's right, as a matter of fact."

"But not close enough for the wives, I've noticed."

Jacques looks up at him over his fast-emptying glass. "That's a very observant young man! It comes from being a photographer, I suppose."

He finishes off his glass and smacks his lips, nodding thoughtfully.

"I hadn't noticed myself, to tell the truth. Well, I guess it takes a little longer with women, they like things to be proper and orderly. They esteem each other a great deal though, those two."

He frowns and narrows his eyes into sagacious slits.

"These etiquette rules are rather tricky sometimes, nobody's sure how to address each other most of the time. Women have a greater natural feel for the right manners. Well, except for Bérengère, of course," he grins, "but that's because I've spoiled her rotten, her mother says. What man in his right mind will marry her, she's always said. Well, here's the answer for her," he pokes at Matt's arm with his empty glass, "*un Ricain* , who doesn't know any better, that's who!" he laughs. It's not just the innkeeper's facial tics that are infectious, Matt reckons.

"Which makes me think," Jacques resumes, after nodding thoughtfully again for a few seconds, "maybe it's time for the two of us to be on a *tu* basis as well. We don't have to wait until we're officially *beau-père* and *beau-fils, n'est-ce pas?*"

Out of the drunken fog that is quickly thickening inside his brain, Matt manages to focus his blurred eyesight on the fuzzy face grinning broadly at him .

That's it? That's all it took?

"*Et ta femme?*" he hastens to ask, "what should I call Hélène? I don't want to seem out of line or disrespectful to her."

Beau-Papa ponders for a second or two, twitching his lips this side and that, the slits of his eyes scanning Matt's face.

"Tricky, *hein?*"

Then he shrugs, averting Matt's avid gaze.

"Just be yourself, *je suppose!*"

TEN

S HE PAUSES IN FRONT of the concierge's door, happy to drop her heavy suitcase for a few seconds. Will Madame Pereira Gonçalves be offended if she doesn't give her one last *bise* before taking off for good? They said all their emotional goodbyes last night, the two of them chatting away for hours in the *loge* like old friends—it seemed like they had been neighbors forever. Back up for her last night in her *chambre de bonne*, she realized there wasn't that much left to cram into her old battered suitcase. Her books had been the first to leave her nest a few weeks ago, her bookshelves she was leaving behind as her own added touch to the small room, along with the blue quilt nicely folded on the armchair under the skyline, her personal gift to the next tenant.

She decides she'll just give the concierge a phone call as soon as she's settled, picks up her suitcase and skulks out, impatient to put the not-so-pleasant details of all this finally behind her—the spooky corridor at the top of the long flight of stairs, the noisy crowd of party animals (friendly of course but—well), the uncomfortable toilet she had to share with them, not to mention the multitudes of flies barging in there nonstop through the cracked window—she laughs, this is all over and done with, as she pulls the heavy door open, struck with exhilaration by the cool gust of wind greeting her outside, yes she is leaving and getting a fresh start, no turning back.

Two kids run past her, late for school, their satchels bouncing on their backs. She watches them waste a few minutes of precious time while the little one refuses to let his barely older sister hold his hand to cross the street. She smiles and walks on, missing the girls already.

Smiling still, she absently meets the eyes of a homeless guy sitting on his regular bench in front of the bakery. He smiles back at her and asks for a cigarette. She doesn't smoke, she answers like always, but this time takes her wallet out to offer him a few euros, her generous goodbye tip to the neighborhood. He nods his thank-you and points at the luggage.

"*Tu pars en vacances?*"

"*Non, je m'en vais*, moving away for good," she says, grabbing her suitcase again.

"Lucky you!"

She looks at his sad ingenuous face, noticing the shave and the fresh haircut, the clean shirt matching the periwinkle blue of his tiny screwed-up eyes.

"I hadn't seen you for a while," she remarks.

"I was at the hospital. They took care of my crazy leg."

He lifts a swollen foot out the loose laces of his left shoe. She doesn't know what else to tell him, then she remembers: "What about your friend, you know the one-eyed man? I haven't seen him around for a while either."

He looks away, then down at his swollen foot. For a second or two he seems to have lost all interest in the conversation, watching his toes stir on top of his gaping shoe, rubbing his kneecap in a slow round motion. She grips her suitcase, wondering what blunder she's just made.

"He comes and goes, you know," he finally answers as she's taken a few steps in the direction of the métro station.

She turns back to wave at him. "Tell him hello from me next time you see him. The American woman. We had a long chat once a few weeks ago. Maybe he remembers me."

"You going back to America then?" he asks, interested again, causing her to pause once more.

"No, I'm only moving over to the left bank."

"Oh yeah, what's there?"

"*Who*'s there, you mean."

He laughs, nodding knowingly. "Tell him to treat you nice." Then holding up his fist with her few euros in it. "I'll drink to your health."

She waves again, unsure what else to say, and moves on.

Yes, she's got somewhere to go and she'd better get there before Luc leaves the apartment for the office. She'll use her time alone to get settled, arrange her books in the new bookcase, on her new desk near the bedroom window, use whatever space he's made for her in the closets, get her bearings in his environment—with this bum's blessings, she smiles.

Odd that this ageless beaten man might very well stand out in her memory when she reminisces about her strange semblance of a life here. Well, she did live here, meet people, talk to some, improving her French. Standing on her stool sometimes in the lonely *chambre de bonne* to look out of the skylight, scanning the patchwork of roofs in their myriad shades of grey under the chang-ing sky and her shifting moods. Hooked on feeling alien, when this guy all along—more or less around all the time but staying put on his bench, with everybody else walking around nonstop, moving in and out of stores, climbing in and out of the métro station, nodding all day their busy hellos to each other–and now she smiles back at the bookseller who is smoking a quick cigarette on his doorstep before opening hours. She did patronize all these shops, paid and took her change, exchanged a few polite words, mingling, for all her reluctance; nobody ever moving away from her in embarrassment, or talking down to her in condescension. She's just been one of them here with her own pleasant enough niche under the roofs. Belonging, somehow. Who has she been kidding, really?

"Anne!"

She stops dead, turns around. Laure, running to her in her heels and tight designer suit.

"I'm so happy to see you," she says in her lightly accented English. "I was going to call you, I have a *big, big* problem." She catches her breath, her hand on Anne's arm. "I had to walk the girls to school, Li Ming is ill. Maybe you could stay one more day? it would be *so, so* nice of you!"

"I'm sorry, Luc's waiting for me, I have to get the key before he leaves for work."

"Maybe you could come back after you get the key, to fetch the girls at school at 11:30?"

"Don't they stay at school for lunch anymore?"

"Not this year, they prefer to eat at home with Li Ming."

"I'm sorry Laure, but I'm going to have a busy day. And I'll be way on the other side of Paris."

"Please. I can't take a day off, I have an important meeting in one hour. *Please.*"

"*Fetch the girls at school at 11:30, then bring them back to school at 13:30*, right?" Anne smirks.

"Yes, please. I'll be back on time tonight to fetch them and take Pauline to her piano lesson."

"You know, I won't be able to do this any longer." Anne shakes her head in subdued exasperation.

"I know, I know. " Laure presses her arm a little more firmly. "Just this one day." Then attempting already a triumphant thank you smile: "It is *so, so* nice of you Anne."

"Tomorrow I'll be out of Paris for my friend Matt's wedding anyway." Two weeks from tomorrow actually, but who needs the exact details right now?

"Of course, of course. It will be fine, my mother is coming." She heaves a loaded sigh of relief, probably the only glimpse of peace of mind she'll get in her roller coaster day.

"I'd better hurry if I don't want to be late for my meeting. Don't forget, 11:30." She is already running down the stairs of the métro station with her halo of posh perfume. "Oh, and Pauline has the key," she remembers before plunging underground.

Anne can't help feeling amused by the cheek of the woman.

And that's when it hits her, uncontrollable laughter gushing to her lips, goofy laughter that gets everybody around staring and frowning at her, standing there in their way right in the middle of the sidewalk with her battered suitcase. Who has she been kidding indeed?

Well, seems after all like she'll have to wait until tomorrow for the actual start of her new life in Paris, to sort out the practical details of her new circumstances, so much to deal with right away, and get down to her new work, whatever it will turn out to be. But what's the hurry now that she's finally left her cell for good?

She grabs her suitcase again and carries it down the métro stairs, bracing herself for the rush hour crowd on one of the worst subway lines in Paris.

About the Author

SYLVIA PARROW lives in Paris, where she has been a resident of the Batignolles neighborhood for the last twenty years. A graduate of Sorbonne University, she teaches English in a lycée (a French high school). *Blue In Grey* is her second novel and a prequel to *Spring Buds*, her debut novel.

About The Publisher

Redmond House Publishing is a Virginia registered company with international offices in Paris, France. We have a passion for publishing books, both fiction and nonfiction, that meet high international book quality standards. Our mission is to provide independent authors with a personal, unique, and more creative way of getting published. We do this by providing our expertise to a small number of selected authors, utilizing our creative and business models to best take advantage of the digital printing and internet-based platforms as well as marketing to brick-and-mortar bookstores and libraries. As authors, computer geeks, experienced business management executives, and publishers, we understand all sides of the business. Our creative team will work alongside our authors to design interesting and exciting concepts and book covers. We also welcome talented first-time authors to be among those possibly selected to work with us, should we acquire your manuscript. Our products and services range from book preparation, editing, cover design, publishing, transcribing to audio formats, printed materials, promo products, customized publicity, concept design and development, and marketing campaigns. We continue to keep abreast of current publishing trends and evolve our techniques and technologies to be at the top of our game.

All of our efforts are directed to getting your book widely and successfully published, marketed, and distributed.